The Big Book of Nutrition for Kids

Eat Smart, Grow Strong

Vandana Verma

DIAMOND BOOKS

www.diamondbooks.in

Publisher : **Diamond Pocket Books (P) Ltd.**
X-30, Okhla Industrial Area, Phase-II
New Delhi-110020
Phone : 011-40712200
E-mail : wecare@diamondbooks.in
Website : www.diamondbooks.in
Edition : 2025
Printed By : Repro (India)

Preface

In a world full of fast food and screen time, it's more important than ever to guide children toward healthy eating habits that will support their growth, strength, and happiness. This book is designed to educate and inspire young readers about the value of good nutrition in a fun, relatable, and practical way.

Aligned with the vision of the National Education Policy 2020 and NCF 2023, this guide empowers students to make informed food choices, understand how their body works, and develop life-long healthy habits. Through stories, activities, and real-life connections, we hope to plant the seeds of wellness in every child.

-Vandana Verma

Foreword

Proper nutrition isn't just about what children eat—it's about how they feel, learn, and grow. As a nutritionist working closely with schools and families, I've seen the power of early food education. This book is a wonderful tool that speaks directly to children in their language. It combines science with storytelling and habits with hope. Let's raise a generation that loves food not just for taste, but for the superpower it gives them every single day.

Contents

Chapter 1

Why Food Matters

Let's Begin- A Story to Spark Curiosity

Aarav and Meher were excited about their school's annual sports day. Aarav stayed up late watching cartoons and didn't feel like eating in the morning. He told his mother, "I'm not hungry," and rushed out without breakfast.

Meher, on the other hand, ate a bowl of oats with banana slices and milk. She packed a fruit for her snack and filled her water bottle before leaving.

By 10:30 a.m., Aarav looked pale and tired. He lost in the first round of the 100-meter race. Meher, on the other hand, felt full of energy. She participated in two races, cheered for her friends, and even helped pass out water bottles to other students.

Their teacher smiled and said, "See how the right food fuels your body? Food gives you power, focus, and cheerfulness!"

Explore – Understanding the Role of Food

What is Nutrition?
Nutrition means getting the right kind of food your body needs to grow, play, think, and stay healthy. It's the science of how food works inside us.

Good nutrition helps:
- Your body grow taller and stronger
- Your brain stay active and focused
- Your skin, bones, and muscles stay healthy
- You fight off illnesses and stay energetic

Why Food is Fuel
Just like cars need fuel to move, our bodies need food. But not just any food — healthy, nutritious food.

Food acts like fuel for our "body engine." It gives us:
- Energy to study, play, and explore
- Strength to build muscles and bones
- Power to think and focus in class
- Protection from diseases

What Different Foods Do

Every food group has a special job:
- **Grains (like rice, bread, roti, oats):** Give energy
- **Fruits and Vegetables (like mango, spinach, carrot):** Give vitamins, minerals, and fiber
- **Proteins (like dal, eggs, fish, paneer):** Help muscles grow
- **Dairy (like milk, yogurt, cheese):** Strengthen bones
- **Healthy fats (like nuts and seeds):** Support brain health
- **Water:** Keeps you cool, helps digestion, and prevents dehydration

Why Too Much Junk Food Is a Problem

Junk food tastes good, but too much of it is harmful. It has lots of added sugar, salt, and unhealthy fat — but very few nutrients.

Too much junk food can:
- Make you feel lazy and tired
- Cause weight gain and tooth problems
- Reduce your focus and energy
- Weaken your body's ability to fight illness

Try It – Activities for You

Activity 1: My Energy Diary

For one day, write down what you ate and how you felt after eating:

Time	What I Ate	How I Felt (Happy, Tired, Sleepy)
Breakfast		
Lunch		
Snack		
Dinner		

Decorate it with food drawings or emoji!

Activity 2: Design Your Healthy Plate

Draw a big circle and divide it into four parts:
1. Fruits
2. Vegetables
3. Grains (like roti or rice)
4. Proteins (like dal or paneer)

Add a glass of water or milk on the side. Color the foods and label them.

Think & Reflect

1. Why do you think Aarav felt tired and Meher felt active?
2. What happens to your body when you don't eat properly?
3. What is your favorite healthy food and why?
4. Do you think what you eat can affect your mood and focus?

Let's Revise – Key Takeaways

- Food gives us energy, strength, and health
- Nutrition means eating the right mix of foods
- Healthy meals help our brain, muscles, and bones
- Junk food should be eaten rarely, not daily
- Drinking water is just as important as eating right

Check Yourself – Quiz Time!

1. What gives your body the most energy?

a) Skipping meals
b) Soft drinks
c) Grains and fruits ✔
d) Watching TV

2. Which food helps you build muscles?

a) Candy
b) Eggs or dal ✔
c) Ice cream
d) Chips

3. Why should we drink water?

a) To avoid food
b) To feel full

c) To stay cool and hydrated ✔
d) To taste sweet

Beyond the Book – Project Time!

Project: "Food = Fuel" Poster
Make a poster showing your body as a machine.

Draw:
- Healthy foods going into your body
- Arrows showing energy, focus, strength, and smiles coming out!
- Label which food helps which body part (e.g., milk = strong bones)

Show your poster to your friends or family and teach them why good nutrition matters!

Chapter 2

Meet the Five Food Groups

Let's Begin- A Colorful School Day

It was "Food Color Day" at school. Everyone had to bring a tiffin filled with colorful, healthy foods. Aarav brought yellow bananas and a boiled egg. Meher brought carrot sticks, chapati rolls, and green peas. Rohan brought sugary cupcakes and fizzy cola.
During lunchtime, the teacher walked around smiling. "Can you find all the food groups in your lunch?" she asked.
Meher's tiffin had four food groups. Aarav had two. Rohan had none.
The teacher explained, "Our bodies need a mix of different types of foods every day. Let's learn about the five food groups!"

Explore – What Are the Five Food Groups?

Food is divided into five main groups. Each group gives your body different nutrients.
When we eat from all five groups in the right balance, we grow well, feel strong, and stay healthy.

1. Fruits and Vegetables – Nature's Colors

Fruits and vegetables are rich in:
• Vitamins (like A, C, E)
• Minerals (like potassium and iron)
• Fiber (helps in digestion)

They help:
• Keep your skin, eyes, and hair healthy
• Boost your immune system
• Keep your tummy happy

Tip: Eat fruits and veggies of all colors — green, red, orange, yellow, and purple — like a rainbow!

Examples:
• **Fruits:** Mango, banana, apple, guava, orange, watermelon
• **Vegetables:** Carrot, spinach, tomato, pumpkin, beans

2. Grains – The Energy Givers

Grains are full of carbohydrates, which are your body's main source of energy.

Choose whole grains more often. They have more fiber and nutrients.

Examples:
• Brown rice, roti (whole wheat), oats, millets, corn, poha, quinoa

Avoid:
• Refined grains like white bread, white rice, and sugary breakfast cereals

Grains help you stay full and active throughout the day.

3. Proteins – The Body Builders

Protein is important for:
• Muscle growth
• Repairing tissues
• Building strong bones and teeth

Examples:
• Dal (lentils), rajma, chana, eggs, paneer, fish, chicken, tofu, soybeans
Even vegetarians can get enough protein by eating a variety of dals, pulses, and nuts.
Growing kids need protein every day!

4. Dairy and Calcium-Rich Foods – Bone Builders

These foods give your body:
• Calcium (for strong bones and teeth)
• Vitamin D (helps absorb calcium)

Examples:
• Milk, yogurt, cheese, buttermilk
• Fortified soy milk or almond milk (for those who don't drink dairy)
Children should have 2 to 3 servings of dairy daily to support growth.

5. Fats and Oils – Good in the Right Amount

Fats are needed for:
• Brain development
• Hormone balance
• Absorbing vitamins like A, D, E, and K

Choose healthy fats, such as:
• Nuts (almonds, walnuts), seeds (chia, flax)

• Olive oil, mustard oil, ghee (in small amounts)

Avoid:
• Deep-fried snacks, packaged chips, and foods with trans fats
Healthy fats are essential, but only in small amounts!

Balanced Plate – What Does a Healthy Meal Look Like?

A balanced meal includes all five food groups:
• ½ plate fruits and vegetables
• ¼ plate grains
• ¼ plate proteins
• Plus a small serving of dairy and some healthy fat

Example Meal:
• Chapati (grain)
• Palak paneer (vegetable + protein + dairy)
• Cucumber salad (vegetable)
• A banana (fruit)
• A glass of milk (dairy)

Try It – Activities Just for You

Activity 1: Food Group Hunt

Open your kitchen cabinets or fridge and list five items. Can you match each one to a food group?

Food Item	**Food Group**
Roti	Grains
Paneer	Protein / Dairy
Tomato	Vegetable
Apple	Fruit

Ghee	Fat

Draw a rainbow using crayons and list one fruit or vegetable of each color.

Activity 2: Make Your Thali
Draw your own Indian-style thali (plate). Divide it into parts and fill it with food from all five groups.
Label them clearly. Add a water bottle or a bowl of curd on the side!

Think & Reflect

1. Which food group do you think you eat the most of every day?
2. Which food group do you forget or skip sometimes? Why?
3. Can you plan a lunchbox that includes all five food groups? Try!
4. Why do you think the food pyramid is wide at the bottom and narrow at the top?

Let's Revise – Key Points

• Our body needs five food groups: Fruits & Vegetables, Grains, Proteins, Dairy, and Fats
• Each group gives different nutrients
• Eating a variety of foods helps us grow, think, play, and stay well
• Balance is the key — not too much of one, not too little of another
• Always drink enough water to complete your plate!

Check Yourself – Quiz Time!

1. What is the main job of grains in your diet?
a) Build bones
b) Give energy ✔
c) Make food colorful
d) Help you sleep

2. Which food is rich in calcium?

a) Rice

b) Apple

c) Milk ✔

d) Onion

3. What's the healthiest way to eat vegetables?

a) Fried in lots of oil

b) Steamed or raw ✔

c) With ketchup

d) From a packet

4. Which food group should you eat the most of every day?

a) Fruits and vegetables ✔

b) Chips

c) Cakes

d) Candy

Beyond the Book – Family Activity!

Create a "Five Food Group Tracker" for your family for 3 days. Make a table and track how many food groups each person eats daily.

At the end of the week, talk about:

- Which food group was eaten the most?
- Which one was missing often?
- What new healthy items can your family try next week?

Stick the chart on your fridge and become the Family Nutrition Expert!

Chapter 3

Rainbow on My Plate

Fruits & Vegetables

Let's Begin- A Fruit Basket Surprise

At lunchtime, Aarav opened his tiffin and found something colorful — red apple slices, green grapes, orange papaya, and some crunchy carrot sticks. "Whoa, it's like a rainbow!" he said.
His friend Rhea smiled, "That's because my mom says, 'Eat the rainbow every day!'"
"Eat a rainbow?" Aarav laughed. "You mean eat colors?"
"Yes," Rhea said. "Fruits and veggies of different colors help different parts of your body. Want to know how?"
Let's explore what these colors mean and why they're so important!

Explore – Fruits and Vegetables: Nature's Superfoods

Fruits and vegetables are some of the healthiest things you can eat.
They're full of:

• **Vitamins and minerals:** for your eyes, skin, brain, and heart
• **Fiber:** which keeps your stomach happy
• **Water:** to keep you cool and hydrated
• **Antioxidants:** that protect your body's cells from harm

What Do the Colors Mean?

Each color group gives your body different health benefits. Here's what the colors on your plate can do for you:

Red (tomatoes, apples, strawberries, watermelon):
• Good for your heart and memory
• Helps fight diseases

Orange (carrots, papaya, oranges, pumpkin):
• Great for your eyes and skin
• Boosts your immune system

Yellow (banana, corn, yellow capsicum, mango):
• Helps with digestion
• Gives you energy

Green (spinach, peas, broccoli, cucumber):
• Builds strong bones
• Keeps your eyesight sharp

Blue & Purple (grapes, blueberries, brinjal, plums):
• Protect your brain
• Help keep memory strong

Tip: The more colorful your plate, the more nutrients you get!

Why Eat Fruits and Vegetables Every Day?

Doctors say children should eat at least:

• 1.5 to 2 cups of fruits per day
• 2 to 3 cups of vegetables per day

That's like eating:
• One big banana
• One apple
• Half a cup of cooked spinach
• A bowl of salad
• And a handful of grapes!

Fresh, Cooked, or Raw – All Are Good!

You can enjoy fruits and vegetables in many ways:
• **Raw:** sliced apples, carrots, cucumbers
• **Cooked:** spinach curry, mixed veg sabzi
• **Juiced:** fresh orange or beetroot juice
• **Boiled or steamed:** peas, broccoli, or sweet corn
• **As snacks:** fruit chaat, veg rolls, smoothies

Try new things! You may discover a new favorite.

But I Don't Like Vegetables!

Don't worry — many kids feel the same.

Try these tricks:
• Mix veggies in pasta, noodles, or paratha
• Add cheese or chutney to taste
• Make veggie faces or colorful salads
• Involve kids in cooking — you may like it more when you help make it!

Fun fact:
It takes up to 10 tries to like a new food. Don't give up!

Try It – Fruit & Veggie Fun

Activity 1: Color Count Challenge

At the end of the day, make a chart like this:

Color	Fruit/Vegetable Eaten Today
Red	
Orange	
Yellow	
Green	
Purple	

Did you eat all five colors? Give yourself a star for each one!

Activity 2: My Rainbow Plate
Draw a plate and fill it with colorful fruits and vegetables. Label each color and food. Use crayons or colored pencils to make it look bright and healthy.
Stick it on your wall to remind yourself to "eat the rainbow" every day!

Think & Reflect

1. What color fruits and veggies do you eat the most?
2. Are there any colors you almost never eat?
3. Why do you think each color helps a different body part?
4. How can you help your family eat more fruits and vegetables?

Let's Revise – Key Takeaways

• Fruits and vegetables are packed with vitamins, minerals, fiber, and water

- Eating a variety of colors helps every part of your body
- Try new fruits and vegetables in fun ways
- The goal is to eat all five colors throughout the week
- Even if you don't like one today, try it again another time!

Check Yourself – Quiz Time!

1. Which fruit is good for your eyes?
a) Apple
b) Carrot ✔
c) Banana
d) Grapes

2. Why is fiber important?
a) For hair growth
b) To make food sweet
c) To help digestion ✔
d) For better sleep

3. What color group protects your brain?
a) Yellow
b) Purple ✔
c) Green
d) Red

4. What should you do if you don't like a vegetable the first time?
a) Try it again later ✔
b) Never eat it
c) Hide it
d) Throw it away

Beyond the Book – Family Fruit Challenge!

Create a Family Rainbow Chart for 7 days.
Each day, all family members write which colored fruits and

vegetables they ate. Use stickers or color pencils to mark them.

At the end of the week:

- Who ate the most colors?
- Who tried a new fruit or veggie?
- What was the tastiest discovery?

Celebrate with a healthy treat like homemade fruit popsicles!

Chapter 4

Grains Give You Go Power

Let's Begin- Race Day Energy

It was Sports Day at school. Aarav was all ready for his 200-meter race. Before the race, he ate a big breakfast of poha, banana, and a glass of milk. His friend Sam didn't eat anything except chips.
When the race began, Aarav ran with great energy and finished second. Sam, however, slowed down quickly and looked tired.
"What gives you so much energy?" Sam asked.
"Grains!" Aarav smiled. "Poha, roti, rice – they give me my go power!"
Let's learn why grains are your body's best fuel!

Explore – Why Grains Are Important

Grains are foods made from cereals like wheat, rice, corn, oats, barley, and millets.

They are rich in:

• Carbohydrates – your body's main energy source

• Fiber – keeps your digestion smooth
• B Vitamins – good for your brain and energy use
• Iron and Magnesium – help blood and muscles work properly

Grains are the "go" foods — they give you the energy to run, think, play, and grow.

Types of Grains

1. Whole Grains

These grains keep all their parts — bran, germ, and endosperm. They have more fiber, nutrients, and are digested slowly.

Examples:

• Brown rice
• Whole wheat (atta) roti
• Millets (bajra, jowar, ragi)
• Oats
• Quinoa
• Barley (jau)

2. Refined Grains

These grains are processed and have fewer nutrients. They digest faster but don't keep you full for long.

Examples:

• White rice
• White bread
• Maida (refined flour) products
• Sugary cereals

Tip: Eat whole grains most of the time. They give you longer-lasting energy.

Common Grain Foods in India

You might already be eating grains every day! Here are some Indian favorites:

- Chapati or roti (whole wheat)
- Rice – brown or white
- Idli and dosa (made from rice and dal)
- Dalia (broken wheat porridge)
- Poha (flattened rice)
- Thepla, paratha
- Bajra or jowar rotis
- Upma
- Khichdi

Grains are not boring — they're in many tasty dishes!

Why Whole Grains Are Better

Whole grains help:

- You feel full for longer
- Your tummy stay clean (thanks to fiber)
- Lower the risk of heart disease and obesity
- Keep your energy steady — no sudden crashes

Think of whole grains as slow-burning fuel — like a power bank for your day!

Try It – Grain Games

Activity 1: Whole vs. Refined

Draw two circles:

- One for whole grains
- One for refined grains

Add food names or pictures to each circle. Then circle the ones you eat often. Are most of them whole grains?

Activity 2: Make a Grain Plate

Create a one-day grain-based meal plan with:
- Breakfast
- Lunch
- Evening snack
- Dinner

Try to include at least three different grains in your plan!

Example:
- **Breakfast:** Oats with banana
- **Lunch:** Bajra roti with vegetables
- **Snack:** Corn chaat
- **Dinner:** Brown rice khichdi

Think & Reflect

1. What grain foods do you eat every day?
2. Have you tried millets like bajra or ragi?
3. How do you feel after eating poha or roti vs. chips or noodles?
4. Can you swap one refined grain with a whole grain this week?

Let's Revise – Key Points

- Grains are energy-givers and full of fiber, vitamins, and minerals
- Whole grains are healthier than refined ones
- Eat a variety of grains like bajra, oats, wheat, and rice
- Grains are found in tasty Indian dishes like poha, chapati, and khichdi
- Choosing whole grains helps you feel fuller and keeps your energy steady

Check Yourself – Quiz Time!

1. What do grains give us?

a) Energy ✔
b) Sugar
c) Protein
d) Fat

2. Which is a whole grain?

a) Maida bread
b) Oats ✔
c) White rice
d) Cake

3. Why are whole grains better than refined grains?

a) They are whiter
b) They have more fiber and nutrients ✔
c) They are cheaper
d) They cook faster

4. Which of these is NOT a grain?

a) Rice
b) Bajra
c) Roti
d) Potato ✔

Beyond the Book – Grain Basket Project

Make a "Grain Basket" at home!

1. Ask your parents to help you collect different grains: wheat, rice, ragi, jowar, corn, oats
2. Label them in jars or boxes
3. For one week, try using a different grain every day in one meal
4. **At the end of the week, discuss:**
   o Which grain tasted best?

- o Which grain gave the most energy?
- o Which one was new to your family?

Bonus: Create a recipe book of grain-based dishes from your region!

Chapter 5

Powerful Proteins

Your Body's Building Blocks

Let's Begin- The Muscle Mystery

Rhea had just finished gymnastics class. She felt strong and proud.
"How do you do those flips so well?" asked Aarav.
"My muscles are getting stronger!" Rhea grinned. "That's what protein does."
"Protein?" Aarav asked. "Like in dal and eggs?"
"Yes," said Rhea. "Proteins are the body's builders. They help you grow tall, stay strong, and repair your body!"
Let's find out what makes proteins so powerful!

Explore – What Are Proteins?

Proteins are special nutrients your body uses to:

- Build muscles, skin, and bones
- Repair wounds or injuries
- Make enzymes and hormones

• Help your immune system fight germs

Proteins are made up of amino acids — tiny building blocks that work like bricks in a wall.

Just like you need bricks to build a house, your body needs proteins to build itself!

Where Do We Get Proteins From?

There are two main sources of protein:

1. Animal-based proteins:

• Eggs
• Chicken
• Fish
• Milk, cheese, yogurt
• Meat

These contain complete proteins — they have all essential amino acids your body needs.

2. Plant-based proteins:

• Lentils (dal)
• Beans (rajma, chana)
• Soybeans and tofu
• Peas
• Nuts and seeds
• Whole grains (like quinoa, bajra)

Vegetarian or vegan? No worries! You can still get all your protein from plant sources by eating a variety of foods.

Why Kids Need Protein Daily

Protein is especially important for children because:

• You are growing quickly

• Your body is active and repairing itself daily
• You need energy for learning and playing
• Your bones and muscles are still developing

Doctors recommend that kids aged 5–13 eat around 4 to 6 ounces of protein per day, depending on age and activity level.

That's about:
• 1 egg = 1 ounce
• ½ cup cooked dal = 2 ounces
• 1 cup milk = 1 ounce
• A handful of nuts = 1 ounce

Combining Foods for Full Power

Some plant foods don't have all amino acids. But when you combine them, you get complete protein!

Try these combos:
• Rice + Dal
• Roti + Chana
• Peanut butter + Bread
• Idli + Sambar
• Hummus + Pita

Tip: Variety is the key! Mix grains, legumes, dairy, and seeds.

Not Enough Protein? What Happens?

If your body doesn't get enough protein:
• Muscles may become weak
• You may feel tired and slow
• You might not grow well
• Wounds may heal slowly
• You may fall sick more often

That's why protein should be part of every meal!

Try It – Protein Power Time

Activity 1: What's on My Plate?

Draw your breakfast, lunch, and dinner plates. Then circle all the protein-rich items you see. Can you add one more protein to each plate?

Activity 2: Protein Tracker
For 3 days, list everything you eat that contains protein.

Day	Protein Foods Eaten (Dal, Egg, Milk, etc.)
1	
2	
3	

At the end, count how many different sources of protein you tried!

Think & Reflect

1. What are your favorite protein foods?
2. Do you eat protein at every meal?
3. Can you swap a junk snack for a protein-rich one like peanuts or curd?
4. Why do athletes need more protein?

Let's Revise – Key Points

- Proteins are building blocks that help you grow and stay strong
- You can get protein from animal and plant foods
- Kids need 4–6 ounces of protein daily
- Mixing different foods gives you complete protein

• Protein helps repair the body, build muscles, and support immunity

Check Yourself – Quiz Time!

1. What does protein do in the body?

a) Builds muscles and bones ✔
b) Gives sugar
c) Helps you sleep
d) Adds flavor

2. Which is a plant-based protein?

a) Chicken
b) Dal ✔
c) Cheese
d) Egg

3. What happens if you don't get enough protein?

a) You grow faster
b) You feel weak and tired ✔
c) You feel more hungry
d) You become taller

4. Which pair makes a complete protein?

a) Rice + Dal ✔
b) Chips + Cola
c) Bread + Jam
d) Pizza + Fries

Beyond the Book – Make a Protein Poster

Create a "Protein Power" poster and include:

• Pictures of protein foods you eat at home
• One fun protein recipe (like peanut curd dip or moong chilla)
• A slogan (e.g., "Power Up with Protein!")

Display it at school or on your fridge to inspire your family!

Chapter 6

Dairy and Its Delicious Duties Strong Bones, Bright Smiles

Let's Begin – Milk Mustache Day

One morning at school, everyone showed up with a "milk mustache" for fun Friday. Aarav had his from a glass of cold milk. Meher brought a banana milkshake. Rhea had yogurt with fruits.
Their teacher smiled, "Looks like today's class is full of calcium superheroes!"
"Calcium?" Aarav asked.
"Yes," said the teacher, "and dairy foods like milk, cheese, and yogurt help your bones grow strong and your teeth shine bright!"
Let's explore how dairy helps us grow healthy and strong.

Explore – What Is Dairy?

Dairy foods come from animal milk. These include:

- Milk
- Yogurt (curd/dahi)

- Cheese
- Buttermilk
- Paneer (cottage cheese)
- Cream and ghee (used in moderation)

Dairy foods are full of calcium, vitamin D, and protein, which are essential for growing children.

Why Dairy Is Important

Dairy foods give your body:

- Calcium – builds strong bones and teeth
- Vitamin D – helps absorb calcium
- Protein – helps muscles grow
- Potassium – good for your heart
- Vitamin B12 – helps your brain work properly

When you drink milk or eat yogurt, you're helping your bones become stronger, your smile brighter, and your growth faster!

How Much Dairy Do You Need?

Doctors recommend:

- Children ages 5–8: 2.5 cups of dairy per day
- Children ages 9–13: 3 cups per day

That's equal to:

- 1 glass of milk = 1 cup
- 1 cup of yogurt = 1 cup
- 1½ slices of cheese = 1 cup
- ½ cup paneer = 1 cup dairy serving

Tip: Spread your servings throughout the day — in breakfast, lunch, and dinner!

Dairy for All – What If I Can't Drink Milk?

Some kids may be lactose intolerant — their body can't digest milk properly.

Don't worry! You can get calcium and vitamin D from:
- Fortified plant-based milk (like soy milk, almond milk)
- Leafy green veggies (like spinach, broccoli)
- Nuts and seeds (like sesame, chia)
- Tofu
- Ragi (finger millet)

Ask your doctor or parents for help picking the right option.

Delicious Ways to Enjoy Dairy

You don't have to drink plain milk every day. Try fun, healthy dairy dishes:
- Fruit + yogurt smoothies
- Flavored milk with cardamom or turmeric
- Paneer sabzi or paneer wraps
- Curd rice or kadhi
- Cheese sandwich with vegetables
- Lassi or chaach (buttermilk) in summer
- Dahi with paratha or poha

Dairy can be tasty AND healthy!

Try It – Dairy Discovery

Activity 1: What Dairy Did I Eat?
Make a 2-day dairy diary:

Day	Morning	Afternoon	Evening
1			
2			

At the end, count how many dairy servings you had.

Activity 2: Build a Bone!
Draw a skeleton with strong bones. Around it, paste or draw pictures of dairy foods and calcium-rich plant foods.

Write one sentence for each: "Milk makes bones strong," "Curd keeps teeth clean," etc.

Think & Reflect

1. Which dairy foods do you enjoy the most?
2. Do you eat dairy with every meal?
3. What do you know about calcium and its role in your body?
4. What could you eat instead of milk if you couldn't drink it?

Let's Revise – Key Points

- Dairy foods are rich in calcium, vitamin D, and protein
- Calcium keeps bones and teeth strong
- Kids need 2½ to 3 cups of dairy daily
- Even if you don't drink milk, other foods can give you calcium
- Dairy can be eaten in fun and tasty ways every day

Check Yourself – Quiz Time!

1. What does calcium do in the body?

a) Helps you see

b) Builds bones and teeth ✔

c) Gives sugar

d) Makes skin soft

2. Which of these is a dairy food?

a) Rice

b) Paneer ✔

c) Tomato
d) Egg

3. If someone can't drink milk, what's a good alternative?
a) Soda
b) Soy milk ✔
c) Jam
d) Butter

4. How many dairy servings do 9–13-year-olds need daily?
a) 1 cup
b) 3 cups ✔
c) 5 cups
d) None

Beyond the Book – Dairy Around the World

Research and make a mini dairy map!
• Find out what dairy products kids eat in Japan, France, India, Mexico, and the USA
• Draw or paste pictures of foods like cheese, yogurt, buttermilk, kefir, paneer
• Present it to your class or family

Extra fun: Try making curd or paneer at home with adult help!

Chapter 7

What to Eat Less Of

Sugar, Salt & Bad Fats

Let's Begin- The Snack Trap!

During recess, Arjun opened his tiffin. It had chips, a chocolate bar, and a fizzy drink. "Yum!" he said.
His friend Meera looked into her box. She had a sandwich, fruit slices, and water.
"Why don't you bring fun snacks like me?" Arjun asked.
Meera smiled. "My mom says too much sugar, salt, and bad fats can harm our health."
Let's uncover the truth about the foods we should eat less of — and why!

Explore – What Are "Sometimes Foods"?

"Sometimes foods" are tasty treats that we should eat only once in a while. These include:

- Sugary snacks (candy, cookies, cake)

• Salty snacks (chips, namkeen, fries)
• Sugary drinks (soda, energy drinks, packaged juices)
• Foods with unhealthy fats (deep-fried foods, pizza, burgers)
• Processed foods (instant noodles, sausages)

They're fun to eat but don't give us many nutrients. In fact, too much of them can cause problems.

The Trouble with Too Much

Sugar Overload

Eating too much sugar can:

• Cause cavities and tooth decay
• Make you tired or hyperactive
• Lead to unhealthy weight gain
• Increase risk of diabetes later in life

Found in: Chocolates, candy, sweet cereal, sweetened drinks
Tip: Look for cereals with less than 8 grams of sugar per serving!

Salt Overload

Too much salt can:

• Raise your blood pressure
• Harm your heart over time
• Cause bloating and thirst

Found in: Chips, sauces, pickles, instant noodles
Tip: Look for "low sodium" or "no added salt" labels on food packets.

Bad Fats

Not all fats are bad! Your body needs good fats like those in nuts, seeds, olive oil, and avocados.

But bad fats like trans fats and too much saturated fat can:
- Block your arteries
- Increase bad cholesterol
- Cause heart disease later in life

Found in: Fried snacks, bakery foods, packaged chips, processed meat
Tip: Avoid foods with "hydrogenated oils" on the label — that means trans fats!

Eat Smart Instead

Instead of unhealthy snacks, try:
- Fruit slices or dry fruits
- Roasted makhana or peanuts
- Whole grain crackers
- Homemade popcorn with little salt
- Fresh fruit juice (no sugar added)
- Curd or buttermilk
- Sprouted chana or moong

Healthy can be fun — and tasty too!

Try It – Swap the Snack!

Activity 1: Healthy Swap Challenge
Match the unhealthy snack to a healthier option.

Unhealthy Option	Healthy Swap
Chips	Roasted chana or makhana
Soda	Lemon water or coconut water
Candy	Dates or raisins
Instant noodles	Vegetable poha
Cake	Banana or fruit salad

Can you create your own swaps at home?

Activity 2: Label Detective
At home, find 3 food packets. Check their sugar, salt, and fat content.

Note:
- Which one has the most sugar?
- Which one is high in salt?
- Are there any with trans fats?

Talk about your findings with family.

Think & Reflect

1. Which snack do you eat the most?
2. Could you eat it less often?
3. What is one fun, healthy snack you enjoy?
4. How can you help your family reduce unhealthy snacks?

Let's Revise – Key Points

- "Sometimes foods" are high in sugar, salt, or bad fats
- Too much sugar leads to cavities and weight gain
- Too much salt can raise blood pressure
- Bad fats harm your heart and health
- Healthy snacks like fruits, yogurt, and roasted nuts are great alternatives

Check Yourself – Quiz Time!

1. What is a "sometimes food"?
a) Apple
b) Chocolate bar ✔
c) Water
d) Dal

2. Which is a healthier choice?

a) Soda

b) Coconut water ✔

c) Candy

d) Cake

3. What happens if you eat too much salt?

a) You become taller

b) You may get high blood pressure ✔

c) You get more energy

d) You sleep better

4. Which is a source of good fat?

a) Fried chips

b) Nuts and seeds ✔

c) Processed meats

d) Butter cake

Beyond the Book – Plan a Healthy Snack Day

Organize a “Healthy Snack Day” at school or at home.

Each child brings:

- A snack with no added sugar
- A drink with no soda or artificial flavor
- A homemade or traditional snack

Create a poster showing your snack and why it’s healthy. Share the fun with friends and family!

Chapter 8

Water – The Wonder Drink for Kids

Let's Begin- The Thirsty Game

On a sunny day, the school playground buzzed with energy. Kids ran around playing football and kho-kho. After a while, Isha sat down, sweating.
"I'm so tired and thirsty," she said.
Her friend Kabir handed her his water bottle. "Water is like magic," he smiled. "It keeps us cool, strong, and full of energy!"
Isha took a big sip and smiled back. "Wow, water is amazing!"
Let's find out why water is the best drink ever for kids.

Explore – Why Your Body Loves Water

Water is essential for life. It helps every part of your body work properly.

Here's what water does:

- Keeps you hydrated

- Helps your brain focus and think
- Keeps muscles working well
- Aids digestion and prevents constipation
- Controls your body temperature
- Keeps your skin fresh and glowing

Your body is made up of about 60% water — that's more than half! So when you drink water, you help your entire body stay healthy and active.

How Much Water Do You Need?

The amount depends on your age, activity level, and weather.

Here's a simple guide:
- Ages 5–8: 5–6 cups per day
- Ages 9–13: 6–8 cups per day
- Ages 14+: 8–10 cups per day

One cup = one small glass.

If you're sweating more or playing sports, you need even more water!

Water vs Other Drinks

Not all drinks are equal. Some give hydration; others can harm if overused.

Drink	Good or Not?	Why
Water	Best!	No sugar, pure hydration
Milk	Good	Calcium and protein
100% Fruit Juice	Sometimes	Natural sugar – limit to 1 cup/day
Soda/Soft drinks	No	High sugar, harmful to teeth

Energy Drinks	No	Not safe for kids
Packaged Fruit Juice	Avoid	Added sugar, low fiber

Water is still the champion!

Smart Water Habits

Here are ways to drink more water every day:

- Carry a water bottle to school
- Drink a glass before each meal
- Add slices of lemon, orange, or cucumber for taste
- Track your water using a sticker chart
- Choose water instead of sugary drinks

Make water drinking fun!

Try It – Water Challenge

Activity 1: Water Tracker Chart
Create a weekly water chart like this:

Day	Glass 1	Glass 2	Glass 3	Glass 4	Glass 5	Glass 6
Mon	✔	✔	✔	✔	✔	
Tues	✔	✔	✔			
...						

Try to check ✔ all glasses by the end of each day!

Activity 2: The Water Taste Test
Try flavored water:

- Add mint + cucumber
- Add orange + lemon
- Add tulsi + ginger

Which one do you like best? Make your own "water recipe" and name it!

Think & Reflect

1. How many glasses of water do you drink daily?
2. What happens when you don't drink enough?
3. Which is better – juice or water? Why?
4. Can you help your family drink more water?

Let's Revise – Key Points

- Water keeps your whole body working well
- Kids need 5–10 cups of water daily
- Water is better than sugary drinks
- Smart habits like carrying bottles and tracking water can help
- You can flavor water naturally for fun

Check Yourself – Quiz Time!

1. What percent of your body is made of water?

a) 30%

b) 60% ✔

c) 90%

d) 10%

2. Which is the best drink for kids?

a) Soda

b) Water ✔

c) Energy drink

d) Packaged juice

3. What happens if you drink too little water?

a) You grow taller

b) You feel tired and may get headaches ✔

c) You sleep better
d) You run faster

4. How can you make water fun to drink?
a) Add candies
b) Add fruits or herbs ✔
c) Mix soda
d) Add salt

Beyond the Book – Create a Water Reminder Poster

Design a poster for your school or home:
• Add fun slogans like “Sip Sip Hooray!” or “Water Your Body!”
• Draw pictures of water bottles, fountains, and happy kids
• List 5 reasons why water is important

Stick it near your dining table or classroom to remind everyone!

Chapter 9

How to Read Food Labels

Be a Smart Food Detective

Let's Begin- Mystery at the Grocery Store

Rehaan loved shopping for snacks. One day, at the supermarket, he picked up a box of colorful cereal and said, "This looks fun!"
His sister Tara looked at the back of the box. "Wait," she said. "It has a lot of sugar and hardly any fiber."

"Whoa!" Rehaan exclaimed. "How did you find that out?"
Tara smiled. "Simple! I read the food label. It tells the real story behind the packaging."
Let's become food detectives and learn how to decode the labels!

Explore – What Is a Food Label?

A food label is the information printed on food packets. It tells you what's inside and how healthy (or unhealthy) the food really is.

Main parts of a label:
1. Nutrition Facts – lists nutrients like sugar, fat, protein, and fiber
2. Ingredients List – shows everything that went into making the food
3. Serving Size – tells you how much one serving contains
4. Allergy Info – warns if the food contains nuts, milk, or other allergens
5. Dates – includes manufacturing date and expiry or 'best before'

Reading labels helps you make better food choices!

Understanding Nutrition Facts

This is usually a small table printed on the back. Here's what to look for:

• Calories – the energy you get from food.
✔ Choose snacks with moderate calories (under 150 per serving)

• Total Fat – avoid trans fats and too much saturated fat.
✔ Choose snacks with good fats and less than 3g saturated fat

• Sugar – the sweet villain!
✔ Try to choose products with less than 8g sugar per serving

• Fiber – good for your tummy!
✔ Choose foods with 2g or more fiber per serving

• Protein – helps in body growth and repair
✔ Look for at least 3g protein in a snack

Ingredients – What's Really Inside?

The ingredients list tells you exactly what went into the product.

Important tips:

• Ingredients are listed in order of quantity – the first ones are in the largest amounts

• Watch out for hidden sugars: glucose, fructose, corn syrup, maltose = SUGAR!
• If the first few ingredients are sugar, refined flour, or oil — not a healthy choice

Rule of Thumb:
Shorter ingredient lists = better

If you can't pronounce the ingredients, it's probably ultra-processed

Label Tricks to Watch Out For

Sometimes packaging tries to trick us. Watch for:
• "Fat-free" – may still have lots of sugar
• "Sugar-free" – might have artificial sweeteners
• "Natural" – doesn't always mean healthy
• "Made with whole grains" – may still be mostly refined flour
Don't believe everything on the front!

Flip the pack and read the label.

Learn the Logo Language

Some food packets show symbols that help us:

Symbol	What it Means
Green Dot	Vegetarian food
Red Dot	Non-vegetarian food
FSSAI Number	Approved by Indian food safety body
"Whole Grain" Badge	Made using whole grains (check % too!)
Recyclable symbol	Good for the environment

Knowing these symbols makes you a smarter buyer!

Try It – Label Detective Mission

Activity 1: Label Hunt at Home
Look into your kitchen. Pick 3 packed foods.

Check and write:
• Calories
• Sugar
• Fiber
• First 3 ingredients
Which is the healthiest? Which has the most sugar?

Activity 2: Supermarket Sleuth

Next time you go shopping, do this:
• Choose 2 cereal boxes
• Read their nutrition labels
• Which one is better? Why?
Present your findings to your class or family like a mini-report!

Think & Reflect

1. Why should we read food labels before eating?
2. What's the harm in eating high-sugar, low-fiber foods daily?
3. What label symbols do you remember?
4. What's one snack you checked today — was it healthy?

Let's Revise – Key Points

• Food labels show what's really inside the food
• Read nutrition facts: check sugar, fat, fiber, and protein
• Ingredients are listed from most to least
• Look for short, simple ingredient lists
• Don't fall for marketing words – check the back label!

Check Yourself – Quiz Time!

1. Which of these means sugar?

a) Corn syrup
b) Maltose
c) Fructose
d) All of the above ✔

2. What's a good amount of sugar per snack serving?

a) 15g
b) Less than 8g ✔
c) 20g
d) None

3. If "sugar" is the first ingredient, what does it mean?

a) It has the most sugar ✔
b) It's sugar-free
c) It's healthy
d) None

4. Which symbol shows vegetarian food?

a) Red dot
b) Green dot ✔
c) FSSAI
d) Chocolate

Beyond the Book – Design a Smart Snack Poster

Create a poster showing:

- How to read a label
- Good vs bad food choices
- Your favorite healthy packed snack with a label sample

Put it up in your classroom or kitchen!

Chapter 10

Building Healthy Habits for Life

Let's Begin- A Habit that Changed Everything

Arjun used to eat chips and cookies every evening. He rarely drank water and skipped breakfast often. He felt tired, got frequent colds, and couldn't focus in school.

One day, his school started a "Healthy Habits Week." He learned to pack fruit in his lunchbox, drink enough water, and eat breakfast daily. In just a few weeks, Arjun felt more active and happier!
What changed? Just his habits!
Let's discover how small daily choices can create a lifetime of good health.

Explore – What Are Healthy Habits?

Habits are things we do again and again, often without thinking. Brushing your teeth, saying thank you, or packing lunch are habits. Healthy habits are daily actions that keep your body and mind strong.

Examples of healthy nutrition habits:
• Eating fruits and vegetables every day
• Drinking 6–8 glasses of water
• Limiting sugary snacks and junk food
• Not skipping breakfast
• Reading food labels
• Eating at the table, not in front of screens

These habits build your immunity, energy, and brainpower.

Why Do Habits Matter?

Good habits make healthy choices easier. When a habit becomes part of your routine, you don't need to think about it — you just do it!

Example: If you get used to carrying a water bottle every day, you'll stay hydrated without reminders.

Healthy habits:
• Prevent lifestyle diseases
• Help you grow properly
• Make you more focused and happy
• Stay with you forever!

Small Steps = Big Change

Start with tiny changes. Don't try to fix everything at once.

Here are some ideas:
• Replace one sugary snack with a fruit
• Drink water as soon as you wake up
• Help set the table for dinner
• Try one new vegetable a week
• Pack a healthy lunch with your parents
The key is to be consistent.

Habits Start at Home

Your home is your first classroom for life skills.
Parents, grandparents, and siblings shape your food habits:
• If your family eats together at the table, you learn to enjoy meals
• If they keep fruits ready, you pick them for snacks
• If they avoid junk food, you do too
You can even be the health hero of your family by setting examples!

Try It – Habit Tracker & Kitchen Helper

Activity 1: Weekly Habit Tracker
Make your own tracker:

Habit	Mon	Tue	Wed	Thu	Fri	Sat	Sun
Drank 6 glasses water	✔	✔		✔	✔		✔
Ate 1 fruit	✔		✔	✔		✔	✔
Ate breakfast	✔	✔	✔	✔	✔		✔

Each tick = a step towards better health!

Activity 2: Kitchen Assistant
Choose one day each week to:
• Help wash vegetables
• Pack your tiffin
• Learn a simple healthy recipe (fruit salad, sprout chaat)
Ask an adult to supervise and be safe.

Think & Reflect

1. What food habit would you like to change or improve?
2. Who is the healthiest person in your family and why?
3. Which new food did you try recently?

4. How can you help your friends make better food choices?

Let's Revise – Key Points

- Healthy habits are simple actions repeated daily
- They improve your mood, energy, immunity, and focus
- Start small – like drinking water or eating breakfast
- Home and family are important for building habits
- A tracker helps you stay on track!

Check Yourself – Quiz Time!

1. What is a healthy habit?
a) Watching TV while eating
b) Skipping breakfast
c) Drinking 6–8 glasses of water ✔
d) Eating chips daily

2. Why are habits important?
a) They help us get lazy
b) They make good choices automatic ✔
c) They are boring
d) They are temporary

3. Which is a good food habit?
a) Eating junk food every day
b) Skipping lunch
c) Eating a fruit daily ✔
d) Drinking soda often

4. How can you build habits?
a) Start small and repeat daily ✔
b) Do everything in one day
c) Wait for holidays
d) Only eat at parties

Beyond the Book – My Healthy Habit Poster

Design a poster that shows:

• 3 food habits you want to improve

• A catchy slogan like "Healthy is Happy!" or "Strong Starts with a Spoon"

• Pictures of healthy actions (drinking water, eating fruits)

Put it up in your room to remind yourself every day!

Chapter 11

Nutrition and Festivals

Eating Smart During Celebrations

Let's Begin- The Sweet Festival Dilemma

It was Diwali, and Aarav's house was filled with delicious smells – laddoos, samosas, kachoris, and sweets everywhere! Aarav was excited, but after two days of nonstop eating, he had a stomach ache and felt tired.

"Why do festivals always mean unhealthy food?" he asked.

His mother smiled and said, "Festivals are for joy and celebration. But we can enjoy them in a healthier way!"

Let's learn how to enjoy our favorite festivals without harming our health.

Explore – What Happens During Festivals?

Festivals are times of:

- Celebration
- Family gatherings

• Special foods
• Less routine

During festivals, we often:
• Eat more sweets, fried food, and snacks
• Skip regular meals
• Watch more TV and play less outside
• Sleep late and wake up late

That's okay once in a while — but if it becomes a habit, it can lead to:
• Tiredness
• Indigestion
• Weight gain
• Weak immunity
So what can we do?

Eat Smart, Celebrate Strong!

Here are some tips to enjoy festivals while eating mindfully:
1. Start your day with a healthy breakfast – like poha, upma, or eggs with toast
2. Stay hydrated – drink plenty of water, coconut water, or lemonade
3. Choose smaller portions of sweets and fried food
4. Balance your meals – if you ate heavy lunch, go light for dinner
5. Add fruits and salads to your plate even during festivals
6. Don't skip meals thinking you'll eat at the party – this leads to overeating later
7. Avoid too many fizzy or sugary drinks

Remember: Enjoy everything, but in balance!

Healthy Festival Treats

Here are some smart swaps:

Instead of...	Try...
Deep-fried samosas	Baked samosas or paneer rolls
Gulab jamun with sugar syrup	Rasgulla in light syrup or fruit yogurt
Creamy sweets	Dry fruits laddoo or dates barfi
Cold drinks	Lemon water, coconut water
Chips	Roasted makhana or puffed rice snacks

You can also make sweets at home using jaggery, honey, or fruits instead of sugar.

Move Your Body – Even During Festivals!

It's easy to forget exercise during holidays.

Try this:

- Dance to festive songs
- Go for a family walk after meals
- Play outdoor games with cousins
- Help decorate or clean the house – it counts as movement!

Your body will thank you!

Involve Kids in Festive Cooking

One of the best ways to enjoy food and nutrition during festivals is by getting involved in cooking.

Kids can:

- Help roll ladoos or cut fruits
- Stir ingredients under adult supervision
- Decorate healthy treats (like fruit skewers or nut bowls)
- Choose the menu with parents – add at least 2 healthy items

This builds a connection with food and gives joy beyond just eating.

Try It – My Festival Food Planner

Activity: Festival Nutrition Tracker
Pick your favorite festival (Diwali, Holi, Eid, Christmas, Pongal, Baisakhi, etc.)
Create a chart like this:

Meal	What I Ate	Healthy Choice Made? (Yes/No)
Breakfast	Poha + banana	✔ Yes
Lunch	Puri, chole, salad	✔ Yes
Snacks	Ladoo + roasted nuts	✔ Yes
Dinner	Rice, dal, paneer	✔ Yes

Now answer:
- Did I eat fruits or veggies today?
- Did I drink enough water?
- Did I enjoy the treats in small amounts?

Think & Reflect

1. Why do we eat more during festivals?
2. What is one smart food swap you can make during celebrations?
3. Which is your favorite festive food – can you make it healthier?
4. How can you stay active during long holiday weekends?

Let's Revise – Key Points

- Festivals are joyful but often come with unhealthy eating
- Smart eating means balance, not restrictions
- Drink water, eat fruits, and move your body
- Involve kids in cooking to make it more fun
- Choose smaller portions and make healthier versions of treats

Check Yourself – Quiz Time!

1. What is a good breakfast during festivals?
a) Only sweets
b) Poha or upma with fruit ✔
c) Cola and chips
d) Cake

2. Why should you drink water during celebrations?
a) To feel full
b) To stay hydrated and prevent tiredness ✔
c) To avoid brushing
d) So you can skip meals

3. Which is a smart food swap?
a) Cold drinks instead of water
b) Roasted makhana instead of chips ✔
c) Creamy sweets instead of fruits
d) Fried snacks every meal

4. How can you be active during festivals?
a) Dancing, walking, or decorating ✔
b) Watching TV all day
c) Sleeping late
d) None of these

Beyond the Book – My Healthy Festival Plan

Make your own festive menu with:
- 2 favorite treats
- 2 healthy dishes
- 1 healthy drink

Draw or write your plan and stick it on the fridge during the next festival!

Chapter 12

Eating for Energy

The Power of Balanced Meals

Let's Begin- Why Am I So Tired?

Riya loved to play badminton after school. But lately, she felt tired before even finishing one game. She was also finding it hard to concentrate in class.

Her teacher asked, "Riya, are you sleeping enough and eating well?"

Riya replied, "I sleep okay, but I skip breakfast and only eat chips and juice during lunch."

Her teacher explained, "Our bodies are like machines – they need fuel to run well. That fuel is balanced meals!"

Let's discover how the right food gives you energy, focus, and strength to do your best every day.

Explore – What Is Energy?

Energy is the power your body uses to:

• Walk, run, jump, and play

• Think and study
• Grow taller and stronger
• Keep your heart beating and lungs working
You get energy from food, especially the nutrients inside it.

Different foods give different kinds of energy:
• Carbohydrates give quick energy (like rice, roti, bread, fruits)
• Proteins build and repair your body (like eggs, dal, paneer, fish)
• Fats store energy for later use (like nuts, seeds, avocado)
• Vitamins & minerals help your body work properly (found in fruits, veggies, dairy)
• Water keeps every cell in your body alive and active

What Is a Balanced Meal?

A balanced meal is a plate of food that includes:
• One source of carbohydrate (like rice or roti)
• One source of protein (like dal, curd, paneer, egg, fish)
• Some vegetables (for fiber, vitamins, minerals)
• A small portion of healthy fat (like ghee, nuts, seeds)
• A drink like water or buttermilk
Think of your plate as a puzzle — all pieces must fit to make it complete!

Balanced meals give you:
• Energy that lasts longer
• Better focus in class
• Fewer cravings for junk food
• Stronger bones and muscles
• A happy tummy and clear skin

When Should You Eat?

The timing of meals also matters:
1. Breakfast – Never skip it! It's your body's first fuel after sleeping

2. Mid-morning snack – A fruit or a handful of nuts
3. Lunch – A full balanced meal with carbs, protein, veggies
4. Evening snack – Choose light options like roasted chana, fruit, or milk
5. Dinner – Not too late and not too heavy

Eating at regular times keeps your energy steady and your digestion healthy.

Sample Balanced Meal Plates

North Indian Balanced Lunch:

- 1–2 chapatis (carb)
- Moong dal or rajma (protein)
- Mix veg or bhindi (fiber and vitamins)
- Curd or chaach (digestion + calcium)
- Fruit like papaya or apple (vitamins)

South Indian Balanced Dinner:

- Idli with sambhar (carb + protein + veggies)
- Coconut chutney (healthy fat)
- A glass of water or lemon juice

Snack ideas:

- Peanut chikki
- Banana with peanut butter
- Sprouts chaat
- Boiled egg and toast

What Happens If You Don't Eat Balanced Meals?

Skipping meals or eating only one food group (like just noodles or just chips) can cause:

- Feeling weak or tired
- Mood swings and irritability
- Constipation or upset stomach

• Trouble focusing in class
• Slower growth or weaker bones

Your body is like a team — it needs all players (nutrients) to win the game of health!

Try It – Build Your Balanced Plate

Activity: My Energy-Filled Day

Draw or describe what you ate today. Then answer:
• Did I include fruits or veggies?
• Did I eat both carbs and proteins?
• Did I drink enough water?
• Was my snack healthy or junk?

Next: Design your own balanced plate using pictures from magazines or drawings. Label each part — carbs, protein, veggies, fats, drink.

Think & Reflect

1. What happens to your energy if you skip breakfast?
2. Can you list one food from each group – carb, protein, fat, vitamin?
3. How do you feel after eating junk vs. balanced meals?
4. What small change can you make today for better energy?

Let's Revise – Key Points

• Food gives you the energy to learn, play, and grow
• Balanced meals contain carbs, proteins, fats, veggies, and water
• Eating regularly keeps your body strong and focused
• Skipping meals or eating only junk food leads to tiredness and poor health
• You can build your own healthy plate every day!

Check Yourself – Quiz Time!

1. Which of these is a source of protein?

a) Chips

b) Paneer ✔

c) Candy

d) Cold drink

2. Why is breakfast important?

a) It helps you sleep

b) It's your first fuel of the day ✔

c) It makes you thirsty

d) It's fun to skip

3. Which meal is balanced?

a) Noodles with ketchup

b) Roti, dal, veggies, curd ✔

c) Chocolate and soda

d) Popcorn and ice cream

4. What does skipping meals lead to?

a) Low energy and poor focus ✔

b) Superpowers

c) Fast growth

d) Extra vitamins

Beyond the Book – Family Food Challenge

Plan a balanced family dinner:

- Assign roles: who cooks, who sets the table, who serves
- Make sure the meal has all 5 parts — carbs, protein, veggies, fat, drink
- Take a picture or draw it!

Discuss at dinner:

- What did we learn about food today?
- How did this meal make us feel?

Glossary of Nutrition Words

Word	Meaning (English)
Nutrition	The process of eating food that helps the body grow and stay healthy
Balanced Diet	A meal that includes all food groups in the right amounts
Carbohydrates	Nutrients that provide quick energy (like rice, roti, fruits)
Proteins	Nutrients that help build and repair the body
Fats	Nutrients that store energy for later use
Vitamins	Nutrients that help in overall body functions and immunity
Minerals	Elements like calcium, iron, and zinc that keep bones and blood healthy
Fiber	The part of food that helps digestion and keeps the stomach clean
Hydration	Drinking enough water to keep the body active and fresh
Junk Food	Food that is high in sugar, fat, and salt but low in nutrition
Calcium	A mineral that helps build strong bones and teeth
Iron	A mineral that helps make healthy red blood cells
Energy	The power your body uses to move, think, and grow
Immunity	The body's defense system to fight illness
Meal Planner	A tool to organize meals in a healthy way
Snack	A small meal between main meals
Digestion	The body's process of breaking down food

✔ Check Yourself – Answer Key

Here are the answers to the quizzes from each chapter:

Chapter 1 – Why Food Matters

1. ✔ b) Food gives us energy
2. ✔ b) Fruits and vegetables
3. ✔ b) Water
4. ✔ a) Makes us weak and tired

Chapter 2 – The Five Food Groups

1. ✔ b) Fruits
2. ✔ a) Protein
3. ✔ b) Milk
4. ✔ a) Water

Chapter 3 – Fruits and Vegetables

1. ✔ b) Carrots
2. ✔ c) All of the above
3. ✔ b) Vitamins and fiber
4. ✔ a) Eat a rainbow of fruits and veggies

Chapter 4 – The Power of Protein

1. ✔ b) Lentils
2. ✔ c) Chicken
3. ✔ a) Grow muscles
4. ✔ b) Fish and tofu

Chapter 5 – Whole Grains for Energy

1. ✔ b) Brown rice
2. ✔ b) Energy
3. ✔ c) Popcorn
4. ✔ a) Oats, roti, and rice

Chapter 6 – Dairy and Strong Bones

1. ✔ b) Calcium
2. ✔ a) Milk, yogurt, cheese
3. ✔ a) Keeps bones strong
4. ✔ b) Drink milk or buttermilk

Chapter 7 – Water: The Magic Drink

1. ✔ a) Keeps our body working well
2. ✔ a) Water
3. ✔ b) 8 glasses
4. ✔ a) Carry a water bottle

Chapter 8 – Smart Snacking

1. ✔ b) Banana
2. ✔ b) Trail mix
3. ✔ a) Gives energy and fills stomach
4. ✔ a) Fruits, milk, dry fruits

Chapter 9 – Sugar and Salt: Handle with Care

1. ✔ b) Sugar and salt
2. ✔ a) Processed food
3. ✔ c) Fruits
4. ✔ b) Check labels

Chapter 10 – Reading Food Labels

1. ✔ b) Energy
2. ✔ a) Ingredients
3. ✔ b) Check calories and sugar
4. ✔ a) Yes

Chapter 11 – Festivals and Nutrition

1. ✔ b) Because food is everywhere
2. ✔ b) Roasted makhana instead of chips
3. ✔ b) Ladoo – make it with dry fruits
4. ✔ a) Dance or walk after eating

Chapter 12 – Eating for Energy

1. ✔ b) Paneer
2. ✔ b) It's your first fuel of the day
3. ✔ b) Roti, dal, veggies, curd
4. ✔ a) Low energy and poor focus